The Three Billy Goats Gruff

Barrie Wade and Nicola Evans

W
FRANKLIN WATTS
LONDON•SYDNEY

Once upon a time there were
three Billy Goats Gruff.

They lived happily in their field, until
they ate all the grass. Then the three
Billy Goats Gruff were very hungry.

They looked longingly across the river bridge. Sweet grass grew in the lush meadow on the other side of the river...

…but a wicked old troll lived under the bridge and he was hungry too. He had often wished the three Billy Goats Gruff would come out of their field.

"I am so hungry!" the littlest Billy
Goat Gruff said to his brothers.
Before they could reply, he clattered
onto the bridge.

At once the troll heard him and raised his massive head. "Who's that trip-trapping across my bridge?" roared the troll.

The littlest Billy Goat stopped short.

"It's only me," he squeaked.

The wicked troll jumped up on the
bridge. He got ready to grab hold
of the littlest Billy Goat.
"I'm going to eat you up," he roared.

"But my brother is much fatter than I am," said the littlest Billy Goat cleverly. "If you are really hungry, you need a good meal."

"Really," said the troll. "You are right.
I suppose I could wait for him."
So he let the littlest Billy Goat cross
his bridge.

Soon the middle-sized Billy Goat clattered onto the bridge.

"Who's that trip-trapping across my bridge?" the troll roared. He jumped up again and blocked the way across the bridge.

The middle-sized Billy Goat

stopped short.

"It's only me," he said.

"I'm going to eat you up!" roared
the wicked troll.
His hands were ready to grab the
middle-sized Billy Goat.

"But my brother is even fatter than me,"
said the middle-sized Billy Goat cleverly.
"He would make you a much better

meal than me."

"Really?" said the troll. "You are right. I suppose I could wait for him." So he let the middle-sized Billy Goat cross his bridge.

Then the biggest Billy Goat left his field
and clattered onto the bridge.

"Who's that trip-trapping across my
bridge?" roared the wicked troll and he
stood in the way of the biggest Billy Goat.

"ME!" bellowed the biggest Billy Goat.

He stamped his hoof.

"I'm going to eat you up," roared the troll, grinning wickedly.

"Oh, no, you're not!" the biggest Billy
Goat roared back.

"Oh, yes, I am!" roared the troll, licking his lips.

Then the biggest Billy Goat snorted,
put his head down and charged fiercely.

He butted the troll up into the air, right off the bridge and into the river. SPLASH!

The wicked old troll sank under the water and was never seen again.

Now all three Billy Goats had crossed over the bridge. They ate the delicious, sweet grass in the meadow...

…and lived happily ever after.

About the story

The Three Billy Goats Gruff is a fairy tale from Norway. The first version of the story in English appeared in 1859, in a collection by George Webbe Dasent called *Popular Tales from the Norse*. Sometimes the goats appear as grandfather, father and son, but more often they are shown as brothers. There are other stories that have a similar plot of "eat me when I'm fatter". Can you think of another one?

Be in the story!

Imagine you are the troll being interviewed by a newspaper. Describe the Billy Goats Gruff.

Now imagine you are the biggest Billy Goat. Describe the troll and explain why you headbutted him off the bridge.

First published in 2014 by
Franklin Watts
338 Euston Road
London
NW1 3BH

Franklin Watts Australia
Level 17/207 Kent Street
Sydney
NSW 2000

A CIP catalogue record for this book is available
from the British Library.

The artwork for this story first appeared in
Leapfrog: The Three Billy Goats Gruff

ISBN 978 1 4451 2835 1(hbk)
ISBN 978 1 4451 2836 8 (pbk)
ISBN 978 1 4451 2838 2 (library ebook)
ISBN 978 1 4451 2837 5 (ebook)

Series Editor: Jackie Hamley
Series Advisor: Catherine Glavina
Series Designer: Cathryn Gilbert

Printed in China

Franklin Watts is a divison of
Hachette Children's Books,
an Hachette UK company.
www.hachette.co.uk

caring for us

I am a Doctor

Deborah Chancellor

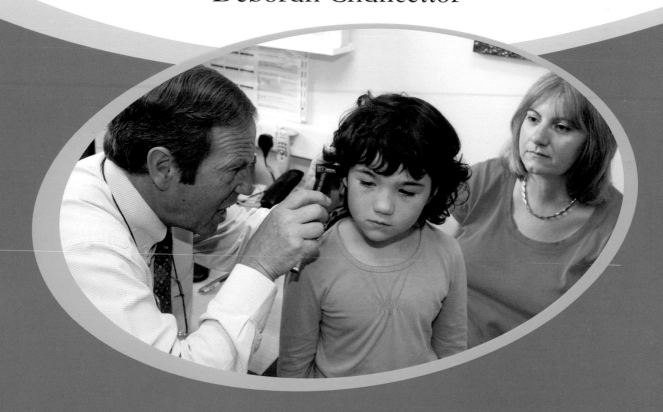

W
FRANKLIN WATTS
LONDON•SYDNEY

This edition 2012

First published in 2010
by Franklin Watts

Copyright © Franklin Watts 2010

Franklin Watts
338 Euston Road
London NW1 3BH

Franklin Watts Australia
Level 17/207 Kent Street
Sydney, NSW 2000

Series editor: Jeremy Smith
Art director: Jonathan Hair
Design: Elaine Wilkinson
Photography: Chris Fairclough

Thanks to Dr Bertram, Hazel, Eileen, Liz, Izzy, Su, Josh and all the staff at Linton Health Centre.

Dewey number: 610.6'95

ISBN: 978 1 4451 0904 6

Printed in China

Franklin Watts is a division of Hachette Children's Books,
an Hachette UK company.
www.hachette.co.uk

Contents

Words in **bold** are in the glossary on page 24.

My job

I am a doctor.
People come to see
me at my **surgery** when
they are not feeling well.
I help them to
get better.

What do you think?

How
can doctors
help their
patients
get well?

I work at a health centre in
a village called Linton.

In the surgery

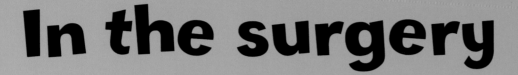

If someone wants to see me, they phone the health centre to make an appointment with the receptionist.

What do you think?

Why do you need to book to see a doctor?

6

My patient list tells me who is coming to
see me that day. I check the **patient notes**
on my computer.

Seeing patients

Every day, I see about 35 patients.
When they arrive, they sit in the
waiting room until it is their turn
to see me.

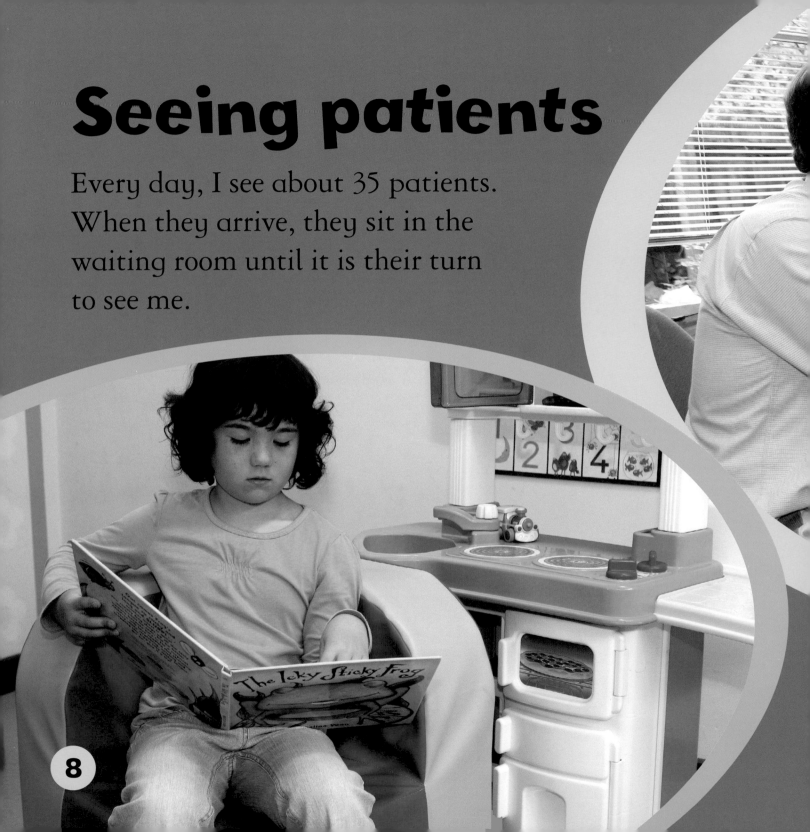

What do you think?

What do you think the doctor is doing in this picture?

In my surgery, I ask my patients how they are feeling and try to help them to relax.

9

What's wrong?

Sometimes I examine my patient to see what is wrong. I may listen to their heart and lungs with a stethoscope.

Do you know?

Colds, coughs and flu are caused by **germs**.

I may look in my patient's ears, and take their temperature with a **thermometer**.

The right medicine

If a patient needs medicine to help them get better,
I give them a prescription.

Do you know?

?

Never take medicine unless a trusted adult gives it to you.

The patient takes the prescription to a **pharmacy**, to pick up the right medicine.

Emergency visit

Sometimes people come to the surgery if they have had an accident, or become ill quickly.

What do you think?

Where else could you go in an emergency?

14

They may need to be taken to hospital to get the right **treatment**. For example, if a patient has a broken arm, they may need a plaster cast.

On the phone

I talk to some patients on the phone if they can't get out to the surgery, but need my advice.

What do you think?

When do you think it's helpful to speak to a doctor by phone?

16

When I am not with my patients, I have a lot of paperwork to do in my surgery.

Out and about

I leave the surgery to visit patients
at home if they can't come out
to see me.

I take my medical case with me when I do a home visit. It contains everything I need.

What do you think?

What kind of patients might need a home visit?

Meeting together

Every day, I meet the other doctors at the surgery to talk about our work.

We work at different times. When I go home at the end of the day, another doctor takes over at evening surgery.

What do you think?

Why do doctors need to talk about their work?

Look after yourself

Eat healthy food to help you stay well. This way you might not have to visit the doctor very often.

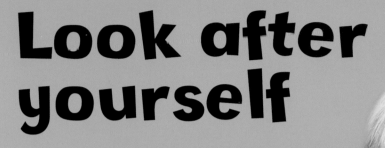

What do you think?

What kind of foods are good for you to eat?

Take lots of exercise to keep fit and strong.
Get plenty of sleep, so your body can rest
and fight germs.

Glossary

germs tiny living things that can make you ill

medicine something you take to help you get better

patient notes information about a patient's medical treatment

pharmacy a place where you can pick up medicine

prescription a doctor's request for medicine

stethoscope a piece of equipment used by a doctor to listen to your heart and lungs

surgery the room where a doctor sees patients

thermometer equipment for measuring your temperature

treatment medical care to help you get better

Index

24